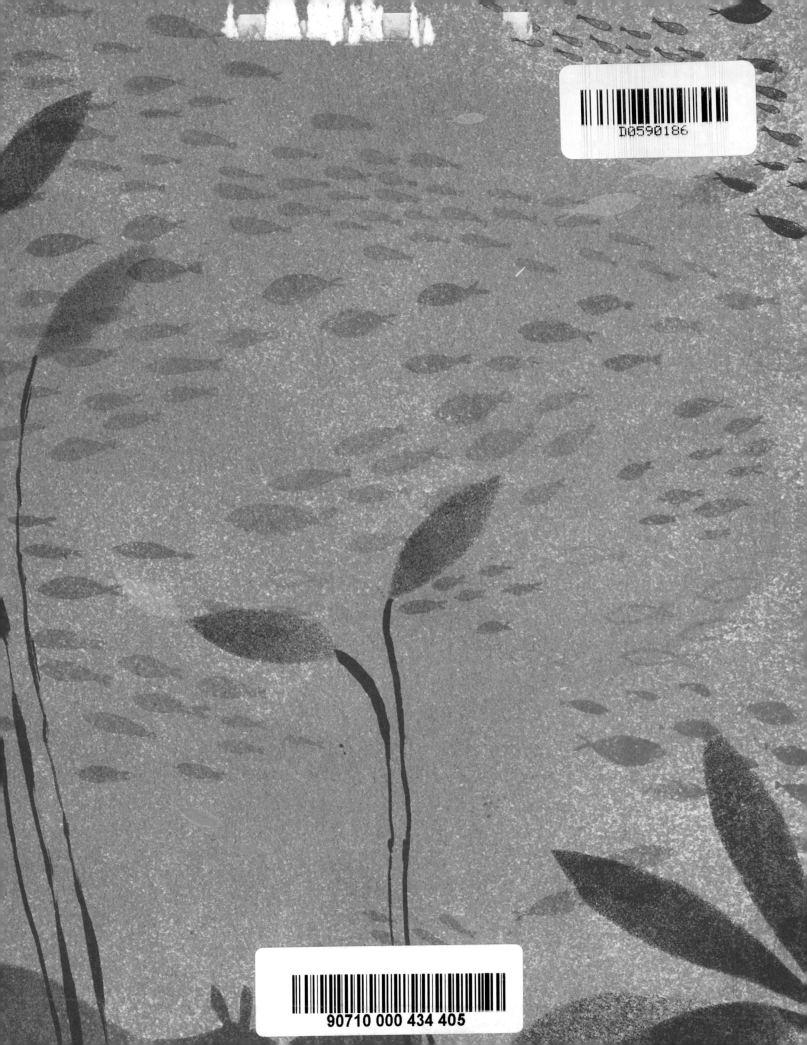

For Luka

WALKER BOOKS
AND SUBSIDIARIES
LONDON · BOSTON · SYDNEY · AUCKLAND

First published 2020 by Walker Books Ltd
87 Vauxhall Walk, London SE11 5HJ

10 9 8 7 6 5 4 3 2 1

© 2020 Anuska Allepuz

This book has been typeset in Didact Gothic

Printed in China

The right of Anuska Allepuz to be identified as author/illustrator
of this work has been asserted by her in accordance with the
Copyright, Designs and Patents Act 1988

British Library Cataloguing in Publication Data: a catalogue
record for this book is available from the British Library

ISBN 978-1-4063-6241-1

www.walker.co.uk

THE WALLOOS'
BIG
ADVENTURE

ANUSKA ALLEPUZ

On a rocky island,
beside a lake,
lived the Walloo family:
Big Walloo,
Spotty Walloo,
Old Walloo
and Little Walloo.

Little Walloo loved to grow the tiny plants that sprouted up in between rocks.

Spotty Walloo loved to cook fresh fragrant salads and soups.

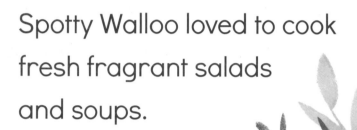

Big Walloo loved to build – boats most of all.

And Old Walloo loved
to tell stories.

"In the old days," he said,
"I would visit tropical-exotic islands –
very BIG ones. You never saw
anything so beautiful!"

Little Walloo loved Old Walloo's stories.
How she wished to have her own adventure ...
to visit a tropical-exotic island herself!

Well, all Walloos love to go on trips ...

so off they went, in a brand new boat built by Big Walloo.

For many days and many nights,
the Walloos sailed bravely across
the wide wild lake.
Until...

"LOOK! LOOK!
A tropical-exotic island!"

Little Walloo's eyes grew wide.
Butterflies fluttered in her tummy.
"Wow-wee!"

The new island was beautiful and lush,
the air moist and fresh,
the plants tall and green.

But Little Walloo had a funny feeling ...
almost as if the land was
rising and falling.

GURGLE!

WURGLE!

GURGLE!

But no one else noticed, as there were so many things to do.

"I will build ten boats for each one of us!" cried Big Walloo.

"I will make the biggest and most delicious tropical-exotic Walloo cakes!" smiled Spotty Walloo.

Little Walloo and Old Walloo
loved wandering
the island together,
collecting seeds.

Over time, Little Walloo and Old Walloo
felt the island was changing.

"Is the island ... hotter?" asked Old Walloo.

"Is the island ... moving?" asked Little Walloo.

They both agreed
something wasn't right...

WURGLE!
GURGLE!

The land *was* moving!
Little Walloo bounced
and bounced
until she landed on ...

a NOSE!

What is this?

Who is this?

"Hello! I'm Little Walloo.
I'm on a tropical-exotic island adventure
with my family!"

"Hello there, little one. I'm Hippo.
I was just about to dive
under the water.
It's far too hot for me
in this scorching sun."

"Where will you go?" asked Little Walloo.

"Where the plants are tall and green,
somewhere that will shelter me
from this burning heat," sighed Hippo.

The Walloos couldn't believe that
the tropical-exotic island was a HIPPO!
They looked around them and felt terrible.
Almost all the plants that had been
around Hippo were gone...

"Please don't leave,"
cried Little Walloo.

She had an IDEA!

Everyone followed Little Walloo's brilliant plan.
Using the leaves they had taken,
Big Walloo and Spotty Walloo
built a parasol for Hippo.

Hippo sighed deeply with happiness.

Meanwhile ...

Little Walloo and Old Walloo spread the seeds
they had collected all around Hippo.

Soon, lots of plants started to grow tall and green
around the tropical-exotic island once more.

The air was moist
and fresh again.

Hippo began to feel
more like himself
under the cool,
sweet breeze.

Now, Little Walloo had lots of stories to tell.
But these were stories that belonged
to them all – Hippo, too.

And with all the beautiful,
lush plants and delicious shade ...

many more hippos arrived!

And Little Walloo had lots of
tropical-exotic adventures
to come with her Walloo family!